Impossible Parents

Impossible
Parents

Brian Patten
Illustrated by Arthur Robins

**WALKER
BOOKS**

For Alice, Max and Sam
B.P.

First published 1994 by Walker Books Ltd
87 Vauxhall Walk, London SE11 5HJ

This edition published 2017

2 4 6 8 10 9 7 5 3 1

Text © 1994 Brian Patten
Illustrations © 1994 Arthur Robins

The right of Brian Patten and Arthur Robins to be identified as author
and illustrator respectively of this work has been asserted by them
in accordance with the Copyright, Designs and Patents Act 1988

This book has been typeset in Garamond

Printed in Great Britain by Clays Ltd, St Ives plc

British Library Cataloguing in Publication Data:
a catalogue record for this book is available from the British Library

ISBN 978-1-4063-7870-2

www.walker.co.uk

CONTENTS

CHAPTER ONE

This is Ben Norm's
bomber jacket.

These are Ben's trousers.

These are Ben's trainers.

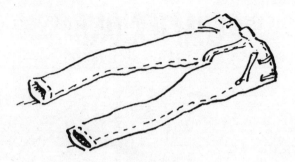

These are his sister Mary's jeans.

These are her boots.

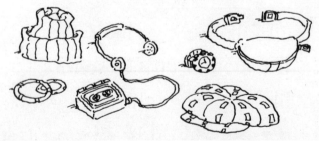

These are some of Ben and Mary's
whatsits.

Put them all together and you can see how good they looked.

Still, Ben and Mary liked fitting in with the other kids in school. They liked wearing the same kind of stuff as their friends, so long as it was fashionable and not *everybody* wore it.

But…

Have you ever seen such a stupid ponytail as this one?

It belongs to their dad and dangles from the back of his head. It's so embarrassing! And it's filthy! If you shook it you'd get enough dandruff to fill a tin of talcum powder!

And what about the daft earring in the corner of his right nostril! It's disgusting!

What happens when he wants to blow his nose? Maybe he can't blow it – ever! Maybe the nose ring gets rusty when he has a cold and his nose drips!

"Ponytails belong on ponies, not adults," snorted Ben.

"And rings belong in bulls' noses, not in grown-ups' nostrils," said Mary. "If it rusts he'll get some dreadful farmyard disease, then he'll have to be put down."

Sometimes – and this is really gross – sometimes when he dressed up, he wore a disgusting multi-coloured SHELLSUIT!

But that wasn't the worst of it. Not only did their dad have a ring through his nose, a ponytail and a disgusting shellsuit, he also wore a puce-coloured bobble hat and a black string vest with holes in it.

"You've got to be really tatty to have holes in a string vest," moaned Ben. "Can you think of anyone who looks worse than Dad?"

"Yes," said Mary. "Unfortunately I can."

This is their mum. In one of her most ordinary outfits. It's a fishnet body stocking! If you think that's weird you should see her when she's dressed for work. You should see what she wears for her job as a belly dancer!

And it wasn't only the way their mum and dad looked.

Dad would pick his nose and
flick bogies at flies. Mum would
practise belly dancing in front of the
window, or take her shoes off and
paint her toenails,
which doesn't
sound so
bad – until
you've smelt
her feet.
Every time
she took her
shoes off, the
cat fainted.

CHAPTER TWO

It was Mary's least favourite person, Alice Frimp, who started all the children boasting about their parents.

"My mum's responsible for keeping the queen's clothes looking fresh. She's a royal fashion consultant," Alice Frimp said in the playground.

"Well, my dad's a test pilot," said Charlie Buggins.

"My mum's a high-powered business woman who used to be a brain surgeon," boasted Mavis Mayhem.

"Mine's an opera singer," said Pattie Rotti.

Mary nearly told the truth. She nearly said her mum was a belly dancer.

Mary thought Alice Frimp was a real grub.

One day, Miss Jones their teacher said, "Don't forget, it's Parents' Day next Friday."

"I couldn't stand Alice Frimp or any of her horrible gang seeing Mum and Dad. They'll poke fun at me for ever. They'll wobble their bellies at me!" wailed Mary as they walked home.

Alice Frimp is real septic.

Ben felt the same. He wished he hadn't said their dad was a fireman. You don't see many string-vested firemen in puce-coloured bobble hats, who have ponytails and wear rings in their noses.

What if Dad absent-mindedly flicked a bogey at Miss Jones? It was the kind of thing he might do. And then he'd pick something from between his teeth – WITH THE SAME FINGER!

Ben and Mary were mortified. Miss Jones would be nice to their parents, and pretend not to notice their nasty habits. But what would she really think, deep down inside?

There must be something they could do to stop the Dreaded Parents coming along to Parents' Day.

It's simple. We won't tell them.

OK. We'll keep Parents' Day a secret.

But their mum and dad already knew.

Every single parent had received a nice letter from Miss Jones.

CHAPTER THREE

That night Ben and Mary held a powwow in their bedroom. The first thing they decided to do was to tackle the problem of Dad.

At midnight, when Mr and Mrs Norm were snoring loudly, Ben and Mary sneaked into their parents' bedroom.

Mary had a pair of very sharp
scissors. A few quick hacks, and off
came Dad's disgusting ponytail.

Ben had a pair of bolt cutters
from the garage. A few expert snips
and off came Dad's nose ring.

Then they took his multi-coloured shellsuit from the cupboard and put it in the dustbin.

That was enough for one night.

When they went down to breakfast next morning, Mr Norm was sitting in the kitchen. He was completely bald and Mrs Norm was busy tattooing his head. She was using a pin dipped in red and black inks. When she'd finished, a blotchy spider's web with a big fat red spider covered his whole head.

"I started losing my hair last night," said Mr Norm, "so I decided to shave it all off and let Mum use my head as a canvas."

"I've always fancied a bit of home tattooing," said Mum.

Ben and Mary were well depressed, but Mr Norm loved the tattoo. He flicked a bogey at a passing fly and sighed with pleasure.

Ben moaned. Mary moaned.
There were only a few days left
before Parents' Day! They were
frantic! Why did they have such
impossible parents?

At school nobody seemed very enthusiastic about Parents' Day. In fact everybody looked a bit worried. Even Mary's arch-enemy, Alice Frimp, who had started them all boasting about their parents, seemed worried.

I don't think my mum will be coming to Parents' Day after all.

I hope... er, I mean I think mine will be away as well.

"I'm looking forward to meeting your dad," said Charlie Buggins. "A real fireman!"

Ben blushed and felt very hot. He wished he'd not told a fib. And Mary nearly burst into tears. Alice Frimp was a triple grub, getting them all boasting!

Mary thought of the horrible humiliation she would feel if it were discovered that her mum was a belly dancer instead of a ballet dancer.

And there was only one day to go!

That night Ben and Mary sneaked back into their parents' bedroom.

They found Mrs Norm's wild blue glitter-wig and hid it behind the wardrobe, along with her disgusting snakeskin belt and her alligator-skin tap shoes.

Next they rummaged about in the cupboard.

They found her fishnet body stocking, which they stuffed into a bin-bag along with her pink feather boa and belly dancer outfit. They threw in Mr Norm's puce-coloured bobble hat and his tatty old black string vest. Then they took the whole lot downstairs and dumped it in the dustbin.

CHAPTER FOUR

When they went down to breakfast next morning, there was a policeman standing in the kitchen talking to Mr and Mrs Norm, who were both wrapped in towels.

"It means I'll have nothing to wear for Parents' Day today!" wailed Mrs Norm.

"Ah, Parents' Day. That might explain a few things," said the policeman thoughtfully.

He turned to Mary and Ben and asked, "Are you two quite sure you don't know anything about this?"

They blushed bright red. Sweat trickled down their sides.

"We often get mysterious goings-on just before Parents' Day," he said. "Well, if I see any suspicious-looking people wearing a glitter-wig, a nose ring and a belly dancer's outfit I'll let you know."

Then he put his notebook away and left.

Mary and Ben were quite pleased
with themselves. Their parents had
nothing to wear now except towels,
and they couldn't very well go to
Parents' Day wrapped in towels.
Ben and Mary left for school that
morning with light hearts.

Two streets away from their house they saw the policeman again. He was peering into a dustbin outside Mavis Mayhem's door.

CHAPTER FIVE

At school everyone looked
happy again. Compared with how
miserable they'd felt after the
announcement of Parents' Day, they
positively glowed.

Everyone looked a bit too pleased
with themselves. They'd all been up
to something, Mary was sure – but
what? Could they possibly have
been trying to stop *their* parents
coming to Parents' Day? Surely not.
Surely nobody else had
impossible parents.
Or did they?

"Quiet, now!"
said Miss Jones.
"You all know
it's Parents'
Day, so I want
you to be on
your best
behaviour."

She looked at her watch. "They're coming soon," she said. Miss Jones seemed to know exactly what the children were thinking. She seemed to know exactly what was going to happen.

Half an hour before the parents arrive...

The children looked out of the windows.

The classroom door burst open and Alice Frimp's mum rushed in. Everyone could tell by the uniform she wore that she worked in the Dry Cleaner's around the corner from Buckingham Palace. So much for her being the queen's fashion consultant! Alice Frimp had fibbed!

But then so had Pattie Rotti fibbed. Her mum wasn't an opera singer.

And Charlie Buggins' dad wasn't a test pilot. He drove the wet-fish lorry. You could tell by the smell.

The parents piled in, one after the other.

Everybody thought everyone else's parents were amazing and wonderful and that only their own were impossible.

Then last of all Ben and Mary's parents stormed in. They had got their clothes out of the dustbin. Mrs Norm wore her belly-dancing costume and everyone thought she was the most amazing mum ever.

Miss Jones was very impressed.
She'd always had a secret desire to
be a belly dancer, so Mrs Norm
showed her how to do it. She stood
up on a desk and did an amazing
dance.

Then Miss Jones tried. She was a
natural.

"I'm giving up teaching this
afternoon and becoming a belly
dancer instead," she shouted. "Let's
all have a party!"

SO THEY DID!

It was the most wonderful
Parents' Day there had ever been.

Brian Patten is one of Britain's best-known poets. His many volumes of adult poetry include *Storm Damage* and *Grinning Jack*, while, for children, he has written the popular verse collections *Gargling with Jelly* and *Thawing Frozen Frogs*. Among his other works for children are the award-winning novel *Mr Moon's Last Case* and the Walker picture book *The Magic Bicycle*.